A Little Moorings PI(

The EASTER Story

Random House/Little Moorings

The Beginners Bible™ and characters licensed exclusively by Performance Unlimited, Inc., Brentwood, TN.

Produced by Don Wise.

The Beginners Bible™ and characters copyright © 1996 by James R. Leininger. All rights reserved under International and Pan-American Copyright Conventions.

Published in the United States by Little Moorings, a division of the Ballantine Publishing Group, Random House, Inc., New York, and simultaneously in Canada by Random House of Canada Limited, Toronto.

Library of Congress Catalog Card Number: 95-072060   ISBN: 0-679-87534-4

Printed in the United States of America   10 9 8 7 6 5 4 3 2 1

LITTLE MOORINGS is a trademark of Random House, Inc.

A celebration, called the festival of the Passover, was about to begin. Jesus told Peter and John, two of his helpers, also called disciples, to prepare a special meal.

"Go to Jerusalem," he said. "You will find a man who will lead you to a house. The owner of the house will show you a large guest room upstairs that we can use."

The disciples did what Jesus had told them, and they found the room—just as he had said. There they prepared the meal.

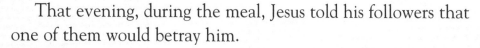

That evening, during the meal, Jesus told his followers that one of them would betray him.

"One of you is planning to do something bad to me," Jesus said.

His friends were surprised to hear this. John was upset. "Who would do this to you?" he whispered to Jesus.

"The man I give bread to is the one who will do it," Jesus quietly answered. Then he broke off a piece of bread and handed it to Judas.

Judas was going to turn Jesus over to the Roman soldiers for 30 pieces of silver.

"Go," Jesus told Judas, "and do what you are planning to do."

After they finished their meal, Jesus took the disciples to a garden.

There Jesus prayed to God because he knew what was about to happen. All of a sudden, soldiers appeared. They were led by Judas.

Judas told the soldiers, "The one I will kiss is Jesus."

Judas went over to Jesus and kissed him.
The guards seized Jesus and took him away.

Jesus was not surprised because a long time ago God had told him that he was going to die this way. Jesus knew that now was the time. God's plan was for Jesus to save people by dying for all the bad things they had done, and would ever do.

The soldiers brought Jesus before their angry leaders. "He must die," the leaders said, "because he says he is the Son of God, and that is against our Law."

So they put Jesus on a cross. And there he died.

The friends took Jesus' body down from the cross. They wrapped him in a clean cloth and laid him in a tomb.

To seal the tomb, they rolled a giant rock across the entrance. The rock was big and heavy! It took many men to move it. Soldiers were placed outside so no one would take Jesus' body.

But early on Sunday morning, the earth began to shake. An angel came down from heaven and rolled the giant rock away from the mouth of the tomb.

The soldiers guarding the tomb were so frightened that they fell to their knees and hid their eyes. "What is happening?" they cried, and then they ran away.

Later that morning, one of Jesus' friends came to the cave.
Her name was Mary Magdalene. She saw that the rock had been
moved away. So she ran to the tomb.

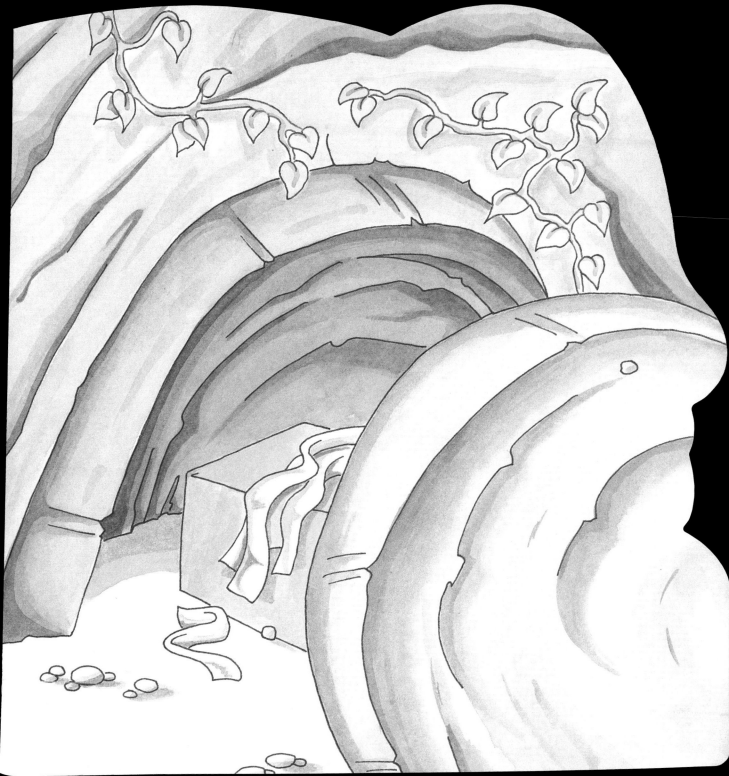

The angel was standing there. But Jesus was gone! "Where is Jesus?" Mary asked the angel.

The angel told Mary, "Jesus is alive! Go and tell all his friends. They will see him again."

Later, Jesus appeared to his disciples and many more people. He told them, "Go out into the world and tell people everywhere about me so they will follow me, too.

"And remember," he told them, "I will always be with you."